PUFFIN BOOKS

THE DISAPPEARING CAT

'I know this secret magic spell. A proper wizard, Walter the Wizard, told me the recipe. It makes people invisible,' said Scott defiantly.

'I bet it doesn't!' said Tracey, suspiciously.

How could it? And yet Tracey decides to see whether Scott is telling the truth. She mixes up the recipe and feeds it to the school cat – which promptly disappears! Tracey is amazed. Then she begins to worry as people find out what she has done, and it looks as though she is going to be in terrible trouble if she can't make the cat visible again!

Poor Sam is in trouble right from the beginning. He isn't really naughty, it's just that being the biggest, tallest boy in Class Six he's often the one to be seen talking or playing around when he should be working. As a punishment, Sam has to miss the swimming lesson, but things turn out quite differently when he makes a daring rescue . . .

The Disappearing Cat and *No Swimming for Sam* are two exciting stories for young readers. They appear together in one volume for the first time.

Thelma Lambert is an artist and designer, and lives in London.

also by Thelma Lambert

NO HOLIDAY FUN FOR SAM
NO PRIZE OR PRESENTS FOR SAM
THE WIZARD PARTY

The Disappearing Cat

Written and illustrated by
THELMA LAMBERT

PUFFIN BOOKS

PUFFIN BOOKS

Published by the Penguin Group
Penguin Books Ltd, 27 Wrights Lane, London W8 5TZ, England
Penguin Books USA Inc., 375 Hudson Street, New York, New York 10014, USA
Penguin Books Australia Ltd, Ringwood, Victoria, Australia
Penguin Books Canada Ltd, 10 Alcorn Avenue, Toronto, Ontario, Canada M4V 3B2
Penguin Books (NZ) Ltd, 182–190 Wairau Road, Auckland 10, New Zealand

Penguin Books Ltd, Registered Offices: Harmondsworth, Middlesex, England

The Disappearing Cat and *No Swimming for Sam* first published by
Hamish Hamilton's Children's Books, 1984 and 1985 respectively
Published in Puffin Books 1986
7 9 10 8 6

Printed in England by Clays Ltd, St Ives plc
Typeset in Linotron 202 Baskerville

Contents

Chapter One

"I can do magic," said Scott.

"Show me then," said his cousin Tracey.

Scott went and fetched a big red box.

"It's a Wonder Wizard Magic Box. I got it for my birthday."

Scott set up a small table and did

some magic tricks. He made ping-pong balls appear from his mouth and playing cards from up his sleeve. Some of the tricks worked, some of them didn't. Tracey was not impressed.

"I don't call *that* magic," she said scornfully. "They're just tricks. I bet you can't do real magic like we saw on T.V. when they made the lady disappear."

"Yes I can!" said Scott. "I know

this secret magic spell, a proper wizard, Walter the Wizard, told me the recipe. It makes people invisible," said Scott defiantly.

"I bet it doesn't! Why haven't you

used it then?" said Tracey suspiciously.

"Well, I'm going to, one day," answered Scott. "But it's not easy to get the things you need for the spell."

"What do you need for your stupid spell, then? I bet there isn't any spell!"

Scott rummaged in the Wonder Box. He produced a crumpled piece of paper.

"Here it is!" he said triumphantly. "Spell to make people or animals invisible. First take one duck's egg and beat well in a cauldron."

"What's a cauldron?" asked Tracey.

"It's what witches mix their spells in. It's a big black pot. Anyway . . . beat well, and add a pinch of salt. Then add two spoons of best sherry and stir, saying the magic words Agga Jiggy Jumbo six times over. The potion is now ready to be given to the one who is to be made invisible." Scott looked up. "That's it," he added.

"Give me the spell, Scotty! I'd like to try it."

Scott hesitated.

"I think you *can* do magic, Scotty," Tracey said quickly.

"Well, you can copy it out. I want to keep the paper as Walter the Wizard gave it to me."

Tracey copied it out into her special notebook.

"I must be going," said Scott.

He took the Wonder Box, and was gone.

Tracey ran to the door. "How do you make them become visible again, Scotty?" she shouted. But Scott did not hear her.

Chapter Two

Tracey would probably have forgotten all about Scotty's magic spell for invisibility if something had not happened.

They were on the kitchen table when Tracey came in from school.

"Mum! What are those enormous eggs? I've never seen any like that in the Supermarket."

"No, Mrs Evans brought them from the farm. Aren't they pretty? They're duck's eggs."

Tracey suddenly remembered the magic spell, 'take one duck's egg,' it had begun.

Tracey went and looked for her notebook. 'I bet it doesn't really work,' she thought. 'It's just one of Scotty's mad ideas. But still, I'd like to try it, just in case.'

Who could she make disappear? Miss Cottrell her teacher? That would be nice. Then she wouldn't have to do that awful maths tomorrow! But perhaps it would be difficult to get Miss Cottrell to take the mixture – and Miss Cottrell could be very nice when she wasn't in one of her strict moods.

'I know,' thought Tracey, 'I'll try it out on an animal.'

Tracey thought of all the animals she knew. Mrs Ryan's bulldog lived across the street, but he was so fierce

that Tracey knew she would never be able to get near enough to give him the magic potion. Mr Wilmott kept rabbits. But Mr Wilmott was a dear old man and he'd be so upset if his rabbits were to 'disappear' and Tracey loved climbing over the back wall and feeding them with lettuce leaves.

Then Tracey remembered the school cat. He was a very fat and greedy tabbycat called Tigger.

Tigger spent all his time fast asleep on a shelf above the radiator outside the school kitchen. He only got down to be fed tasty kitchen scraps by Mrs Munn.

Tracey read the spell again. 'Beat well in a cauldron.' Well a jam jar would have to do. 'A pinch of salt.' That was easy. 'Two spoons of best sherry.' Tracey knew her mother kept a bottle of sherry for making sherry trifle which was her father's favourite pudding.

Tracey mixed up the spell and beat it well with a wooden spoon, saying the magic words six times as she did so. She poured the eggy mixture into a jam jar, put on the lid and hid it in her school bag.

'Tomorrow I'll give this to Tigger. Then we'll see if Scotty's magic really does work!' Tracey said to herself.

Chapter Three

Next morning Tracey was the first child through the entrance at Hill Street School. She paid her dinner money and hung up her coat. Then she took the jam jar and went to the school kitchen. Sure enough, there was Tigger in his usual place, fast asleep on the radiator shelf.

Tracey tipped the magic potion into a plant pot saucer and pushed it temptingly near him. Tigger jumped down and began to eat greedily. In his hurry he got the eggy mixture all over his whiskers. He had nearly finished when the kitchen door opened and Mrs Munn appeared.

"What are you doing here dear? Shouldn't you be in your class?"

"Yes, Mrs Munn," said Tracey. "I'm just going."

Tracey told her best friend Kate Webb all about the magic spell for invisibility. The news spread quickly round the class. There was a buzz of excitement.

"Settle down," cried Miss Cottrell. "What's the matter with everyone?"

Ben Philips put up his hand. "Please Miss, Tracey can make people invisible."

"She's got a magic spell," chipped in Sam Reeve, "she's making the school cat disappear!"

"Now stop talking nonsense and get out your Maths books." Miss Cottrell was in one of her strict moods.

By morning break everyone knew the whole story: how Tigger had been fed a real magic potion and was probably now invisible. A group of excited children went down to the kitchen. It was true. The shelf where Tigger always slept was now empty!

Tracey gulped. She was half-pleased, half-horrified that Scotty's magic potion had really worked.

"You'll get into terrible trouble when Mrs Munn finds out," said Ben Philips. Everyone turned to gaze at Tracey.

"Yes, terrible trouble! She loves that cat."

"Perhaps he's not really invisible,"

said Tracey miserably. "Perhaps he's gone into the kitchen."

They all trooped outside to gaze in through the steamy windows of the school kitchen. Mrs Munn's two

helpers were chopping carrots and peeling potatoes, and there was a big black pot of stew bubbling on the stove. There was something sticking out of the top of the pot . . . it could have been a spoon handle, or . . .

"It's Tigger's tail! He's fallen in the stew!" shouted someone excitedly.

"No, he hasn't! He's been made invisible. He ate the magic spell and he's invisible, I tell you!"

Everyone had their own idea as to what had happened to Tigger.

"Well I'm not eating school dinner today," announced Sam Reeve. "I'm not eating Tigger stew!"

"Nor am I!" said a dozen voices.

They gazed in at the kitchen window again, and pressed their noses to the glass to get a better view. Mrs Munn was now stirring the big black pot with a huge wooden spoon. When she saw the row of faces pressed against the window, she waved them angrily away.

It was Sam Reeve who saw them first.
A line of muddy cat-paw prints
meandering across the playground.

Class 4 followed the trail eagerly. It
led them to Mr Cooper's garden shed.
In the gloom they could see spades

and flower pots and a broken netball post, but no Tigger.

"I can hear snoring!" said Kate Webb.

Someone else claimed to hear scratching noises.

"Here you lot – clear off!" Mr Cooper suddenly appeared, wielding a big broom.

"But Mr Cooper, there's an invisible cat in your shed," began Ben Philips. "We heard him mewing."

"You'll be mewing in a minute mate. Now hop it!" Mr Cooper gave them a friendly sweep with his big broom and the children scampered off.

They gathered in a corner of the playground to discuss the matter.

"Well, if Tigger has been made invisible by Tracey's magic spell, she'll just have to unmagic him," said Ben Philips.

They all looked at Tracey accusingly. "Yes, unmagic him. We don't want him invisible."

Tracey looked worried. "But I don't know how to!" she wailed.

"Well find out how. Remember Tracey Robinson, we want our cat back!"

"You've got until dinner time to get him back," said Ben Philips sternly.

Chapter Four

Tracey had to find her cousin Scott
and get the other part of the spell – to
make invisible things visible again.

Scott was in Class 6, the top class
in the school. They were doing a
special project, measuring the school
playground. Tracey crept up to him,

hoping that Mr Marshall wouldn't
see her.

"Scotty!" hissed Tracey. "You
know that invisible spell you told me
– the one you got from Walter the
Wizard? Well I tried it out on Tigger,
and it worked. And now I want to
unmagic him – everyone wants him
back. They say unless they're sure
he's not in the stew-pot, they won't
eat school dinner today. So you see,

34

I've *got* to get him back to prove he's
not in the stew, and . . ."

Scott put down his measuring
string. "Hey! What are you jabbering
on about?" he said.

When Tracey had explained it all
again, Scott opened his eyes wide.
"Well! I never thought it would really
work!" he murmured. "The spell to
make him reappear was on the
other side of that paper which Walter

the Wizard gave me. I think I can remember it. 'Take a string of sausages, and say the magic words six times backwards and . . .' " Just then, Mr Marshall noticed that Scott wasn't measuring the playground, but was chatting to his cousin. He started to come over so Tracey raced away.

Tracey wondered how she could get a string of sausages? Then she remembered; tomorrow was Thursday, which was bangers-and-mash day. There would be sausages in the larder, waiting to be cooked for tomorrow's dinner. But how to steal them from under Mrs Munn's nose?

Tracey slipped back to Class 4 and told Kate Webb the problem. Kate said she could lure Mrs Munn out of the kitchen for a minute on some false errand and then Tracey could slip in to the larder and get the sausages.

"What can I say to call Mrs Munn out?" wondered Kate.

"I know, say the gerbils are loose in Class 4 and Miss Cottrell says can you come and help catch them?" said Tracey.

"Will it work?" said Kate.

"It's got to," said Tracey. "But it would be better if we really let the gerbils out of their cage."

"What are you two chatting

about?" asked Miss Cottrell, glaring at them over her glasses.

"Nothing Miss."

And so the plan was carried out. Tracey let the gerbils out of their cage and they ran around the classroom and everyone began to scream. Miss Cottrell screamed louder than anyone

else. Kate and Tracey slipped out in the general pandemonium and headed for the school kitchen.

"Mrs Munn! Mrs Munn! the gerbils are loose in Class 4 and Miss Cottrell says could you come and help her catch them?" Kate said breathlessly.

Mrs Munn dropped her wooden spoon and dashed out. Tracey slipped into the big cool larder with its marble topped shelves. And there, sure enough, were the lovely strings of sausages. Tracey ran out, a string of sausages flying out behind her.

She said the magic words backwards, and left the sausages on the shelf by Tigger.

"I only hope this unmagics him," she prayed.

Chapter Five

Peace reigned once more in Class 4.
Mrs Munn had captured Jack and
Jill, the gerbils, and Miss Cottrell had
calmed down. Heads were bent over
work books and you could have heard
a pin drop it was so quiet.

The bell sounded loud and clear.

"Dinner time, Class 4," cried Miss

Cottrell brightly. "I think we all need it today, to steady our nerves!"

"I'm not eating cat stew," muttered Ben Philips.

"Well, let's see if Tigger is back," said someone else.

They all hurried down the corridor to the kitchen. Tracey squeezed to the front of the crowd. The sausages had gone, every single one. And Tigger was back, looking fatter and lazier than ever, fast asleep on the radiator shelf.

"He's back! He's back! Not invisible any more!"

Everyone stroked Tigger and made a big fuss of him. The tabby cat

opened his green eyes sleepily and
wondered why he was suddenly the
centre of all this attention.

Tracey heaved a sigh of relief.

"I'm starving!" said Ben Philips. "The dinner bell's gone ages ago."

For lunch there was delicious creamy mashed potato, carrots, peas, and the stew from the big black pot. Then there was treacle pud and custard. Everyone had seconds.

"That was the best school dinner I've ever had," sighed Kate Webb. And Tracey agreed with her.

Mrs Munn came out of the kitchen to give Tigger his dinner time scraps. "There you are my love," she said with her big jolly smile.

But Tigger didn't move. He was deeply asleep. The occasional twitch of a whisker was the only sign of life.

"That's the first time ever that Tigger's not eaten his dinner. I hope he's not sickening for something." And Mrs Munn went back into the kitchen shaking her head.

Chapter Six

Scott hadn't done his maths home-
work. He'd been watching T.V. with
his young cousin Tracey.

"You'll get into trouble with Mr
Marshall," said Tracey. "You'd better
do it."

Scott frowned.

"Why don't I become invisible

instead? Then when the maths lesson is over, I'll become visible again."

Tracey stared. "You mean . . ."

"Yes, take Walter the Wizard's spell myself. It worked on Tigger didn't it?"

Tracey opened her eyes wide. "You'd never dare," she said.

Next day at school, Tracey looked for Scott in the playground.

"Scotty? No, he's disappeared. I don't know where he is," said his best friend Steve.

No one seemed to know. Had he really made himself invisible?

Tracey called at his home on the way back from school. Her Aunt

Irene opened the door. She told her that Scott had been very sick indeed after breakfast.

"Come in and cheer him up, Tracey love," she said. "He's feeling very sorry for himself."

Scott was lying on the sofa in the sitting room. He looked as pale as a sheet. While Aunt Irene was in the

kitchen making the tea, Tracey ques-
tioned her cousin.

"Scotty! Did you really take the
magic spell?"

"Yes – it tasted awful! It didn't
work at all – it just made me sick. I
don't know how that cat ate it – he
must have a stomach of iron."

Aunt Irene came in with the tea

things and Scott's medicine. "This pink stuff the doctor's given you works like magic," she said.

At the word magic, Scott groaned. And the two cousins agreed to leave magic well alone in future.

No Swimming for Sam

Written and illustrated by
THELMA LAMBERT

For Margaret Maskell

Chapter One

Sam was the biggest, tallest boy in the class. Although he was only seven he took the same size shoes as his teacher, Miss Barker. Being big was good in some ways: in games, he could run faster; in assembly he could see over everyone's heads. But it also had its drawbacks. Being big, Sam

always got noticed. If some boys were mucking about, Sam would be the only one spotted from the staff-room window. If quiet was asked for, it was always Sam who could be seen, head and shoulders above everyone else, still talking.

One day Miss Barker said she had some good news for Class Six. They were to start swimming lessons the next week.

"We'll be going to the Community Centre swimming pool. Have any of you been there?" No one had.

"We're very lucky to be allowed to use the pool, as it's really for the handicapped people who go to the Centre. So we must all be very well-

behaved indeed, do you understand? The water is extra warm, too . . ."

Miss Barker said she would be taking them every Tuesday and everyone must bring a swimsuit and towel in a plastic bag. She said there would be a proper swimming teacher, Mrs Tompkins, to teach them to swim.

"Now, girls, bring swimming hats if you've got long hair, and everyone wear nice easy clothes without too many buttons and things so you can get dressed quickly afterwards. And remember, as a treat there'll be hot cocoa instead of milk when we get back to school—SAM! What ARE you doing!" cried Miss Barker. "Sit down at ONCE!"

Sam was standing on a table by the window, straining to see something.

"Miss!" he cried excitedly. "There's a robin's nest in that oak tree! I've just seen the mother robin going in—"

"Sam! Have you heard a word I've said?" sighed Miss Barker.

Chapter Two

Sam lived in a block of flats with only his Auntie Kathleen and Uncle Dennis. They were kindly people, but rather older than his friends' mums and dads. Since he retired, Uncle Dennis had become a keen model builder, and one whole room in the flat was given over to his model village. Uncle Dennis spent most evenings tinkering about with it, adding bits here and there and inventing new lighting effects.

It wasn't until Monday evening, just at bedtime, that Sam remembered about swimming in the morning.

"Auntie! I've got to take swimming things tomorrow, Miss Barker said! Where are my trunks?"

"Oh, Sam! Why didn't you tell me before? I don't know where they are. We haven't had them out since the Isle of Wight . . . "

After searching high and low, they found his old tattered swimming trunks. Sam struggled to get them on.

"Auntie Kathleen, these trunks are

too small for me; I can't get them on!" he groaned.

It was true. They slowly split down one side as he gazed down at them.

"Oh dear!" sighed his aunt. "What shall we do? I know, you're nearly as big as your Uncle Dennis. Try his on."

She held up a huge pair of old-fashioned swimming shorts smelling strongly of moth-balls.

But they were no good, no good at all! They were far too big. Sam had to hold them up with both hands or they fell down to his ankles!

Auntie Kathleen laughed.

"Here, you can't swim in those, it's indecent! We'll just have to buy you a new pair on Saturday."

"Now hands up, who hasn't got their swimming things?" said Miss Barker on Tuesday morning.

One hand went slowly up: Sam's.

He explained his problem, and how they were going to buy a new pair of swimming trunks at the market on Saturday.

Miss Barker sighed. She was really very fond of Sam, but he did always make extra work, somehow.

"Well, you'll just have to watch quietly this time, Sam."

Soon a neat crocodile of children set off for the Community Centre, all swinging their plastic bags. All except Sam, that is.

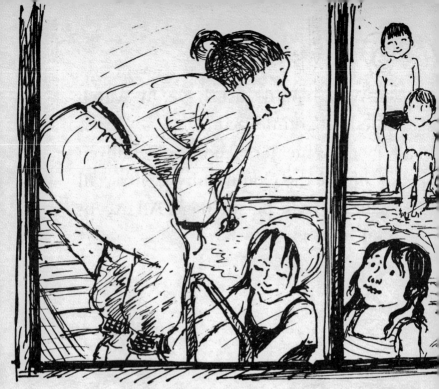

Inside they were met by Mrs Tompkins, the swimming teacher, a very large lady with a loud, jolly voice.

While the others were undressing in the changing-rooms, Sam sat where Miss Barker had told him, on a wooden bench.

The class were all in the water now,
he could hear them laughing and
splashing. The sounds were muffled,
as there was a heavy sliding-door of
glass to shut the pool off. Sam
watched through the glass wall, sunk
in gloom . . .

"Hello, Sam!"

Sam looked round.

Near by was a small group of people in wheelchairs, making things out of wood.

"Hello, Bill!" Sam smiled. "What are you making?"

Sam went to talk to his friend.

Bill lived on the ground floor of Sam's block of flats.

Bill was carving a big piece of wood into a horse's head.

They chatted for a while, and Sam began to cheer up. He told Bill about the swimming trunks, and about finding the robin's nest. Bill let Sam have a go with his chisel.

"I like talking to you, Sam. Not

many of the children come and talk to
me, but you always do."

Just then a ball bounced over to

them, and they saw it had come from the toddlers' Play Group in the next area.

A little girl of two or three came running across to get the ball. It had rolled under the bench, and Sam got

it out for her. She skipped back to the
Play Group.

"They shouldn't come into this
area—it's dangerous for little children, some of them are only babies,"
said Bill.

They watched the children for a while, playing with the sand and the bricks and paints.

Then Sam told Bill all about Uncle Dennis's model village, and the time passed quite quickly. Soon Mrs Tompkins was opening the heavy sliding-door and Class Six came out, wet and happy after their first swimming lesson.

"See you next Tuesday, everyone," boomed the large Mrs Tompkins heartily.

Chapter Three

On Saturday Sam went to buy the new swimming trunks. They took the bus to the market, and found some very smart red stripey ones. They were marked age 10–11 but Auntie Kathleen thought they'd fit.

"I've got some super new swimming trunks," said Sam when they got home.

"You'll be the smartest boy in that swimming pool!" said Uncle Dennis. "Let's see them, then!"

But to Sam's horror, he realized he'd left them on the bus! He'd been helping his aunt with the heavy shopping bags full of carrots and potatoes and things and put his paper bag down on the seat . . .

"Oh, *Sam* . . . " sighed Auntie Kathleen.

"I'll take him to the depot. I expect they've been handed in," said Uncle Dennis. "Cheer up, Sam!"

Uncle Dennis had been a bus driver before he retired, so he knew all the people down at the bus garage.

There was a place there marked
LOST PROPERTY.

"Hello, Ted!" said Uncle Dennis to
the small, smiling man behind the
counter. "Young Sam here has left
something on the 31 bus this morning. Anything been handed in?" he
winked, and Ted winked back.

OPENING
TIMES
MON-FRI
10 — 6
SAT & SUN
2 - 4

"Well, let's see . . . I'll just go and look . . . "

Ted came back with—a set of false teeth! He snapped them up and down, as if they were eating.

"It wouldn't be these now, would it, Sam?"

Sam shook his head.

"No? Well, maybe . . . " He disappeared and came back with a stuffed owl in a glass case, which he put carefully on the counter beside the false teeth.

"This, perhaps? This lovely snowy owl . . . No? Or this bust of Queen Victoria—" whipping out a small statue from the shelf under the counter.

"Have people really left all this

stuff on buses?" said Sam, gazing
enviously at the stuffed owl.

"Now, Ted, have another look.
Isn't there a brown paper bag with a
pair of red stripey swimming trunks
inside?"

Ted disappeared for the last time

and came back with an even bigger smile on his face.

"Would this be the thing you left on the 31 bus this morning?"

Ted pulled out the swimming trunks and held them up.

"Yes, yes, YES!" cried Sam happily. "Now I can really go swimming on Tuesday!"

And Sam and Uncle Dennis skipped all the way home.

Chapter Four

When Class Six got to the Community Centre the next Tuesday the swimming pool door was closed and there was no Mrs Tompkins.

Miss Barker took the children to the sitting area where there were sofas and tables.

"Wait here quietly, everyone, while

I find out what's happened to Mrs Tompkins."

Sam sat next to little Benny, the smallest boy in the class and his best friend. They soon became bored and restless.

It was little Benny who spotted it. A red painted handle, high up on the wall.

"Bet you can't reach that," said Benny.

"Bet I can," said Sam.

"Bet you can't."

"Bet I can!"

Sam reached up and pulled.

What he hadn't done was read the words under the handle:

IN CASE OF FIRE PULL HARD

A dreadful deafening, jangling noise filled the Community Centre. People began rushing about, and suddenly Miss Barker and Mrs Tompkins appeared, both shouting, "What on earth has happened?" above the din.

"It was Sam, Miss! Sam pulled the alarm bell!" cried Benny, pointing his

finger at Sam, now cowering behind a sofa.

The caretaker was found, and he stopped the bell ringing.

"You NAUGHTY boy!" cried Miss Barker. "NO SWIMMING FOR SAM today!"

So once again, poor Sam was on the wooden bench, and this time he felt even gloomier than before.

Bill called out to him, "What! No swimming for Sam again? Never mind, come and see how my wood carving's coming along!"

The wooden horse's head was almost finished now, and Bill was sandpapering it.

"You can do the ears if you like," said Bill.

Sam sandpapered away for a bit, but his heart wasn't in it. He could see all his class-mates in the shimmering blue water of the pool. They were at the far end, swimming through big hoops held by Miss Barker and Mrs Tompkins. Sam could hear their laughing and splashing clearly today, as the sliding-door had been left open.

Sam went and sat on the bench again, feeling hot and miserable; how he wished he was swimming with the class!

Idly he watched the Play Group children. The mothers were drinking cups of tea and coffee, deep in conversation . . .

Suddenly, quick as a flash, a little

red-haired girl of about three streaked past him and through the open door of the swimming pool. To Sam's amazement, she toddled straight in

and was flat on her face floating in the water! And no one but Sam seemed to have seen it happen.

Sam stood up and opened his mouth, but no sound came out. Without stopping to think he rushed in after her.

Sam waded in, and even though he couldn't swim, thanks to his height he could go in up to his chest and reach her. He grabbed the straps of her dungarees and with all his strength he hauled her out, a dripping, spluttering bundle.

The little red-haired girl ran screaming for her mother, and Sam was left standing there, wet through and feeling rather dazed.

Suddenly everyone noticed him.

"SAM! WhatEVER are you doing NOW?" shrieked Miss Barker. "Can't you read the notice? THIS DOOR TO BE KEPT CLOSED!"

Miss Barker seemed to think that

Sam had opened the sliding-door and had come in to lark about!

Poor Sam was still too shaken up to protest his innocence.

Miss Barker was hustling him out, scolding all the while, when a loud voice rang out.

"I say! I saw the whole thing! I saw Sam save a little girl's life!"

It was Bill. He had seen it all from his wheelchair.

Miss Barker made him tell her exactly what had happened: how the little girl from the Play Group ran in through the open door into the pool, and how Sam rushed after her and dragged her out of the water, saving her from drowning.

"And *who* opened the sliding-door?" cried Miss Barker.

There was a short silence.

"Mrs Tompkins did," chirped little Benny. "Mrs Tompkins said it was too hot in here. She said she wanted some air . . . "

Mrs Tompkins went very red, and

didn't know what to say, except, "Thank you," very softly. Not in her usual cheerful, hearty voice, but quietly. "Thank you, Sam."

The next day at school, Miss Barker brought in pink iced buns and fizzy lemonade, and they had a little party.

She said it was in honour of the hero of the swimming class: Big Sam, the LIFE-SAVER!

didn't know what to say, except, "Thank you," very softly. Not in her usual cheerful, hearty voice, but quietly. "Thank you, Sam."

The next day at school, Miss Barker brought in pink iced buns and fizzy lemonade, and they had a little party.

She said it was in honour of the hero of the swimming class: Big Sam, the LIFE-SAVER!

Also in Young Puffin

NO HOLIDAY FUN FOR SAM

Thelma Lambert

Will Sam have any fun on holiday?

When Sam sees the words NO BUCKETS AND SPADES IN THE HOUSE in his hotel, he knows he's in for a dismal holiday. Kippers for breakfast and pouring rain...will he ever survive it? Adding to that, Sam's cub pack plan to go camping in Wales. Sam is really excited at the idea, but well-laid plans can go wrong...

Also in Young Puffin

No Prize or Presents for Sam

Thelma Lambert

Sam has always wanted a pet of his own.

Sam sets out to get himself a pet to enter in the Most Unusual Pets Competition at the village fête. But the animal he chooses leads to some very unexpected publicity.

Sam decides it is up to him to give his Aunty and Uncle a happy Christmas when his Aunty loses her job. But how can he earn some money?